LITTLE SIMON
An imprint of Simon & Schuster Children's Publishing Division • 1230 Avenue of the Americas, New York, New York 10020 • First Little Simon hardcover edition August 2015 • Copyright © 2015 by Simon & Schuster, Inc. All rights reserved, including the right of reproduction in whole or in part in any form. LITTLE SIMON is a registered trademark of Simon & Schuster, Inc., and associated colophon is a trademark of Simon & Schuster, Inc. For information about special discounts for bulk purchases, please contact Simon & Schuster Special Sales at 1-866-506-1949 or business@simonandschuster.com. The Simon & Schuster Speakers Bureau can bring authors to your live event. For more information or to book an event contact the Simon & Schuster Speakers Bureau at 1-866-248-3049 or visit our website at www.simonspeakers.com.
Designed by Laura Roode. The text of this book was set in Usherwood.
Manufactured in the United States of America 0715 FFG
10 9 8 7 6 5 4 3 2 1
Library of Congress Cataloging-in-Publication Data
Green, Poppy. Looking for Winston / by Poppy Green ; illustrated by Jennifer A. Bell. — First Little Simon paperback edition. pages cm. — (The adventures of Sophie Mouse ; #4) Summary: "Sophie Mouse's brother, Winston, wants to help her build a fort in the woods, but Sophie Mouse tells him he should go home because he's too little. When she realizes that she could use his help, he's nowhere to be found!"— Provided by publisher. [1. Brothers and sisters—Fiction. 2. Missing children—Fiction. 3. Mice—Fiction. 4. Animals—Fiction.] I. Bell, Jennifer (Jennifer A.), 1977- illustrator. II. Title. PZ7.G82616Lo 2015 [Fic]—dc23 2014043214
ISBN 978-1-4814-3004-3 (hc)
ISBN 978-1-4814-3003-6 (pbk)
ISBN 978-1-4814-3005-0 (eBook)

the adventures of
SOPHIE MOUSE
4
Looking for winston

By Poppy Green • Illustrated by Jennifer A. Bell

LITTLE SIMON
New York London Toronto Sydney New Delhi

Contents

chapter 1

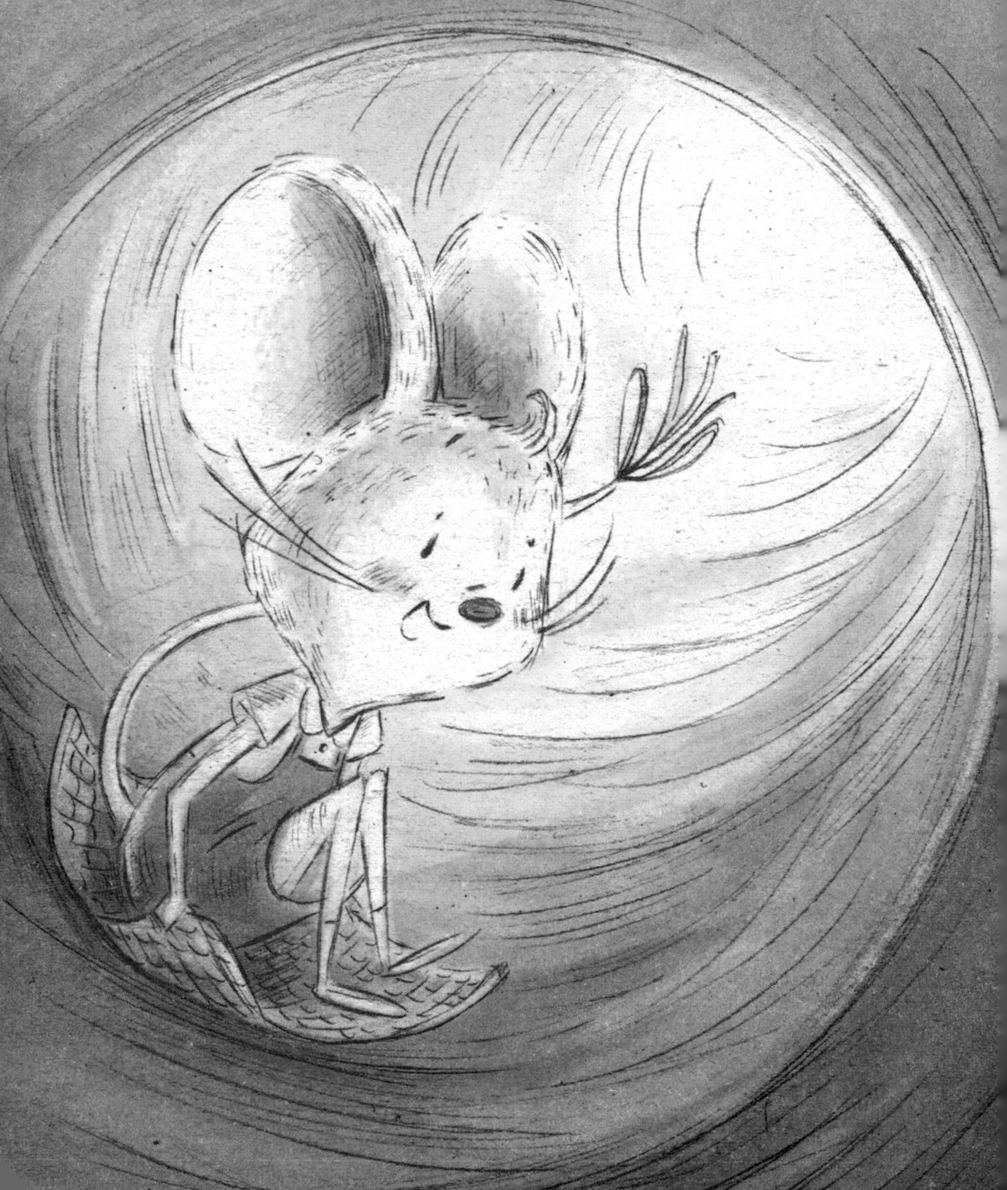

Fun with Friends

"Wheeeeeeeeeeee!" Sophie squealed with delight. Her voice echoed off the curved wooden walls of the giant tunnel slide. Sophie slid through the darkness. The slide twisted to the right. Then it turned to the left. Sophie grasped the fern she was sitting on. The slide track spiraled around and down, down, down, until—

Sophie came shooting out of the bottom end. *Fwomp!* She landed in a soft pile of green leaves.

High above, on a birch branch, Sophie's best friends cheered.

"Whoo-hoo!" cried Hattie Frog.

"Wow!" Owen Snake called out. "That's a long way down!"

Birch Tree Slide was a hollow, twisted branch. It leaned up against the trunk of a

huge birch tree. To get to the top of the slide, Sophie, Hattie, and Owen had first climbed way up the tree using its knotholes. Sophie had been excited to go first.

Hattie came down next. She disappeared into the tunnel. Sophie could hear her whooping all the way down. At the bottom, Hattie landed

next to Sophie in the leaves. They both laughed.

Sophie and Hattie had found Birch Tree Slide together when they were six years old. It felt like their secret place. Sophie had shown it to her brother, Winston. Hattie had shown it to her big sister, Lydie.

Now they had brought Owen. He

and his family had moved to Pine
Needle Grove a while ago. But there
were still lots of fun places Owen
had never been.

"Come on, Owen!" Sophie
called up. "Your turn!"

Owen didn't look so
sure. He stayed coiled up,
not moving. He seemed to be mea-
suring the slide in his
head.

"It's so much fun!" Hattie shouted. "We promise!"

Finally, Owen disappeared into the slide. Sophie could hear an "Aaaaaaaaah!" that sounded far away but grew louder and louder.

And then—*whoosh!*—there was Owen, jetting out of the bottom of the slide. His face looked panicked as he flew through the air. But when he hit the leaf pile—

Owen burst out laughing. "That is
so fun!"

"Isn't it?!" Hattie cried.

Sophie patted Owen on the back.
"Told you we'd have fun this weekend. Didn't we, Owen?"

The three friends had decided on

a project for the weekend: to take Owen to as many new places as possible.

Just then, a blue butterfly fluttered out of the trees. It circled Owen's head once, then flew on.

"Wow, what kind of butterfly was that?" Owen asked.

Hattie's brow wrinkled. "Probably a blue morpho."

"That reminds me," Sophie said with a gasp, "Owen hasn't been to Butterfly Brook!"

Hattie jumped up. "Oh yes!" she cried. "We have to take you there. It's the prettiest spot. And lots of different kinds of butterflies live there!"

"Sometimes," Sophie said, "if you are very still, they will land in your hand." Sophie glanced at Owen and quickly added, "Or on your head!"

Owen laughed. "I want to see it! Why don't we go tomorrow? Right after breakfast?"

Sophie frowned. She had chores to do after breakfast. "You two go on together in the morning. I'll do my chores fast and meet you there."

chapter 2

Sophie's Dream House

"Sorry I'm late!" Mrs. Mouse called. She had just stepped through the front door. "The bakery was so busy today!"

Sophie, Winston, and their dad were already sitting down at the table for dinner. Mr. Mouse had made spaghetti squash and a kale salad.

"I have something to add," said

Mrs. Mouse. She pulled a loaf of cranberry-nut bread from her bag. "Just out of the oven!"

Sophie's nose twitched and she smiled. She loved having a mom who owned a bakery!

"So what did I miss?" Mrs. Mouse asked.

Mr. Mouse served her salad. "I was just telling Sophie and Winston all about my new project," he said.

"I'm going to design a house for a turtle family."

"Guess what the best part is, Mom!" Sophie said.

But Winston couldn't wait for her to guess. He blurted out the answer. "They want it to look like a turtle shell on the outside!"

"Winston!" Sophie scolded. "I said for her to guess."

"Sorry," Winston mumbled. "I couldn't help it."

Mr. Mouse was an architect. He designed homes for animal families all over Silverlake Forest. Sophie loved to watch him do sketches at his drafting table. She thought she might like to design a house someday. Or maybe it would be even more fun to design a *play* house—or a fort! What would it be like, Sophie wondered. A little cottage with comfy chairs and reading nooks? A tree house with

ladders to go up and slides to come down? Or maybe a breezy, floating boat-fort on a babbling brook? Which reminded her . . .

"Hattie and I are taking Owen to Butterfly Brook tomorrow," Sophie

shared. "And I just decided: I think we should build a fort there!"

It would be the perfect spot—a fort in the woods that no one would know about. Well, except for Sophie's parents and Winston.

After dinner, Sophie sat on the couch reading a book. Winston sat next to her, tying knots in a long reed. He'd been doing that a lot lately.

Winston was trying  to earn his knot-tying badge in Junior Forest Scouts.

"Sophie," said Winston, "can I come with you tomorrow to help build the fort?" He smiled up at her sweetly.

Sophie frowned. She didn't want to hurt Winston's feelings. But he *was* only six. She worried that he would get in the way.

"Sorry, Winston," Sophie said gently. "But you're too little. Building a fort is hard work." Seeing Winston's

smile disappear, she added, "How about this? I'll bring you to *see* the fort when we're all done. Okay?"

Winston looked down and nodded. He went on tying knot after knot without saying another word.

chapter 3

Footsteps in the Forest

Leaves crunched under Sophie's feet. It was still early in the morning. But Sophie's chores were done and she was already halfway to Butterfly Brook.

She shifted her satchel to her other shoulder. Inside she had water and snacks and her painting supplies— some brushes and berries. Sophie always brought art supplies with her in case she saw something she just *had* to paint. She was already thinking about the scene she'd paint after they finished their fort today.

Step by step, Sophie's feet carried her closer to Butterfly Brook. She

thought about the advice her dad had given her about building.

"Try to use your strongest materials at the bottom of the structure," Mr. Mouse had said the night before. "And don't forget about windows! Light is important."

Sophie pictured a fort with a skylight— a big window in the ceiling. *Could we make something like that? Or maybe a fort with hanging vines for walls, so you could walk right*

through them! Or an underground fort with tunnels. Or—

"Ouch!" cried a little voice.

Sophie stopped in her tracks. Who had said that?

She looked all around and up into the trees. But Sophie didn't see anyone. All she heard now was a cricket chirping.

She shrugged and kept walking.

Crunch, crunch, crunch went the leaves under her feet. She walked and walked. Then, between two of her steps, she thought she heard other footsteps behind her.

Sophie stopped. The other footsteps stopped too. She turned.

There was no one there.

Sophie's fur pricked up on her

back. There was no reason to fear other animals in Silverlake Forest. But Sophie did feel like someone was following her. Why would they be hiding?

She walked on, faster this time. Faster and faster still. Then, suddenly, she whipped around.

This time, she saw something.

A flash of gray disappeared behind a tree trunk. Sophie stood still, staring in that direction. As she looked more closely, she could see it.

A little mouse tail was sticking out from behind the tree.

Sophie marched over. "Winston!" she said. "What are you doing here?"

Winston was

crouched down behind the tree. He stood up and smiled sheepishly at Sophie.

"You followed me?" Sophie asked her brother.

Winston nodded. "I wanted to

come and help build the fort," he said. "Can I? Pleeeease?"

Sophie sighed. "Do Mom or Dad know where you are?" she asked. "You can't just run off without telling them."

Winston nodded again. "Right after you left, I told them I was going with you. I ran to catch up." He looked down at the ground. "But I knew if you saw me, you'd tell me to go home."

Just then, Sophie noticed a scrape on Winston's knee.

Winston saw Sophie looking. "I

tripped over a tree root," he explained.

Ah-hah! thought Sophie. That was the "ouch" she'd heard.

Sophie opened her bag. She took out her water canteen and a handkerchief. She wet the handkerchief and used it to gently clean Winston's scrape.

"Winston," she said, "I told you. You're too little to help us. You need to go home and take care of your knee." She handed the handkerchief to Winston. "Here. You can take this with you."

Winston started to argue. "But I—"

"No buts!" Sophie said, putting on her best big-sister voice. "I told you not to come along. But you did any-way and *now* look. You need to go home, Winston."

Winston's shoulders fell. He kicked at some leaves. "You never let me go

anywhere with you," Winston said
as he shuffled away.

Sophie put her hands on her hips.
"That's not true!" she called.

But Winston didn't answer.

— chapter 4 —

Butterfly Magic

Sophie turned and stomped toward Butterfly Brook. Sometimes Winston was so frustrating!

How is he supposed to help us? He's already hurt. What if he got even more hurt? I'm just looking out for him.

Still, Sophie felt bad. She knew there *was* another reason she didn't want Winston to come.

We'd spend more time looking after Winston than we would building. That wouldn't make any sense at all!

She walked and walked, but Sophie couldn't shake it. She kept thinking of the sad look on Winston's face.

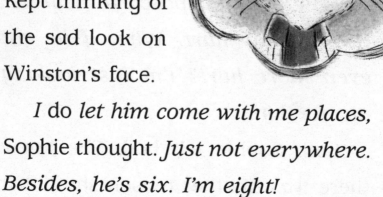

I do *let him come with me places,* Sophie thought. *Just not everywhere. Besides, he's six. I'm eight!*

At Butterfly Brook, Sophie met up with Hattie and Owen.

"You were right," said Owen, looking around. "This is amazing!"

Sophie's frustration with Winston faded as she looked around too. She had been here so many times. But it still felt magical to her. The

water in the narrow brook skipped
down the rocks. On either side of the
brook, evergreen trees grew in the
dappled sunshine. The trees' long
lower branches arched down toward

the ground. They created little hideaways underneath.

Sophie and Hattie led Owen to
one of the hideaways. They peeked
in. Dozens of butterflies fluttered in

the small space. There were bright
yellow ones, orange ones, and blue
ones, too.

"Blue morphos!" Owen whispered, pointing them out.

"Right!" whispered Hattie. "There are tons of different kinds of butter-flies here. They seem to like hiding out here under the branches."

The three friends watched the butterflies for a little while. Then they stepped out from under the branches.

Sophie rubbed her hands together. "So, I have an idea!" she said. "What do you say we build a fort—right here at Butterfly Brook?" Sophie told Hattie and Owen about the house her dad was designing for the turtle family. "It really got me . . . *inspired!*" Sophie said dreamily.

"I'm in!" said Owen.

Hattie nodded. "Let's do it!"

"All right!" said Sophie, clapping with excitement.

"I've been thinking about how we can build it."

Hattie laughed and gave Sophie a friendly squeeze. "Why am I not surprised?" she said.

chapter 5

The Design

They didn't waste any time. They scanned the area for building materials. They found lots of pine boughs on the ground.

"Maybe good for the roof!" Owen suggested.

They found plenty of rocks—large and small—on the bank of the brook.

"We could use these for the

foundation," said Hattie.

"Great!" said Sophie. "My dad did say to use the strongest materials at the bottom." Sophie stood and looked around. "But what we really need for the structure of the walls are a few sturdy sticks."

They searched and searched. Almost all the sticks and branches

on the ground
were the bendy
pine kind.

Finally
Owen called out,
"What about these?"

He had found two
long sticks under some leaves.

"I think they're perfect!" Sophie
said. "I wish there were more. But
maybe we could make a lean-to."

"A *what*-to?" Owen asked.

Sophie laughed. She walked over
to an evergreen tree. "My dad taught
me that a lean-to is usually a building

that is made when two things *lean* against something else. So we could lean our two sticks against this trunk," she said, patting the tree trunk.

"Oh! I get it," said Hattie. "The sticks would make our frame. And we can tie the pine boughs over the frame to make the walls!"

"Yes!" Sophie and Owen cried together.

They agreed on a plan. Hattie and Owen would gather as many pine boughs as they could. Meanwhile, Sophie would go find something they

could use to tie them together. She
knew where to find some reeds. She
walked downstream to gather them.

When Sophie got back, she had a
bundle of reeds.

"Let's see if this will work!" Sophie said.

Hattie held a bunch of pine boughs together. Sophie wrapped a reed around them. But when she tried to tie it, the knot slipped out.

Sophie tried again. Again, the knot slipped.

Hattie and Owen tried too. They tried double knots. They tried triple knots. But nothing worked.

"These reeds are too slippery," said Owen.

All of a sudden, Sophie thought of someone: Winston! He was a Junior Forest Scout. He had been learning to make all kinds of knots. Sophie bet he could tie a knot in the reed that would *stay* tied.

Plus, Sophie knew how much Winston wanted to build with them. He would be so excited to help out!

Sophie told Hattie and Owen her idea. They agreed it was great, and Sophie scurried home to find Winston.

She ran the whole way, smil-
ing. She imagined what she'd say—
"Winston, we need you!"—and she
imagined the look on Winston's face.
Maybe he would even admit that
Sophie *did* let him do stuff with her.

Sophie was out of breath as she

ran into their house in the roots of the big oak tree. "Winston!" she called out. "WIN-ston!"

There was no answer. The house was silent. Sophie quickly checked upstairs. But she could tell right away, the house was empty.

Where was everyone? Where was Winston?

— chapter 6 —

Missing Mouse

Sophie spotted a note on the toad-stool table.

Dear Sophie,

When you and Winston get home, come find me at the library. I'll be working there this afternoon. Mom is at the bakery.

Love,
Dad

Sophie twirled her tail as she thought. Her dad must have left the note before Winston came back. Otherwise, it would say he *and Winston* were at the library.

So when Winston got home, no one was here, thought Sophie. She looked down at her dad's handwriting. *And Winston can't read cursive.*

Where would Winston have gone?

Probably to his favorite place, thought Sophie. The playground! It wasn't far. Their parents let him go there on his own. One day the week before, Winston had run off to play there before he'd even had breakfast. *Mom sure wasn't happy about that!* thought Sophie.

Sophie scurried down the path toward town. Before the first bend, she ducked down a side trail. It twisted through some maple trees. Then it came out into a big clearing—the playground.

Two of her rabbit friends from school were there. James, who was Winston's age, was on the rope swing. His big brother, Ben, was on the monkey bars. It was a small playground, but there was also a seesaw, a

climber, and a line of tree stumps
that Winston liked to hop across.

Sophie said hello. "Have you seen
Winston?" she asked.

Ben and James shook their heads.
"No," said James. "We've been here
all morning. He hasn't been here."

"Hmmmmm," Sophie said. "Okay. Thanks."

Sophie paused to think about where to check next. Maybe by the stream near Hattie's house? Tall reeds grew along the bank. Winston had been going there a lot to get reeds to practice tying knots.

Sophie scurried over to the stream. But Winston wasn't there, either.

Sophie tossed a pebble into the stream. The water rippled out from the splash. *Where else could Winston be?* she thought. *He wouldn't have gone to the bakery to find Mom. It's too far and he's not allowed to go alone. And he doesn't know Dad is at the library.*

Suddenly Sophie noticed an older toad sitting on the bank downstream. She was reading the newspaper. Sophie hurried over to her.

"Excuse me," Sophie said politely. "Have you seen a little spotted mouse this morning?"

The toad looked up from her paper. She studied Sophie. "Seen one?" she said. "I'm looking at one right now!"

Sophie laughed. "No, I mean smaller than me," she said.

The toad put her paper down. "Well, now. I do recall seeing a mouse

earlier. I'm not sure, but I think he went that way." The toad pointed downstream.

Sophie gasped. "He did? Oh, thank you. Thank you so much!"

She skipped along downstream, happy to have a lead. She'd catch

up with Winston. She'd give him the good news. And she'd get him to come back to Butterfly Brook.

chapter 7

A Few Clues

At the next bend in the stream, Sophie had to slow down. The bank was muddy. She had to choose her path carefully. She looked down to plan her hops from rock to rock.

That's when she spotted them.

Fresh tracks in the mud!

Sophie stopped. She looked more closely. Yes! She was sure, now. They looked like mouse tracks!

Now I'm definitely on the right path! thought Sophie. *I will follow these mouse tracks wherever they lead. And at the end, I will find Winston!*

So Sophie followed the tracks. She followed them down the stream. They led to a spot where a log foot-bridge crossed the water.

Muddy mouse footprints led across the bridge. So Sophie crossed the bridge too.

On the other side, she found more tracks in the mud. And that wasn't all. Sophie spotted a little pile of nut shells between two of the footprints. Acorn shells! Winston's favorite!

The footprints and the trail of

acorn shells led upstream, so Sophie followed them along the stream bank. Finally, the tracks took a turn away from the water. They led out of the mud and into a thicket. On the firmer ground, Sophie couldn't see the tracks anymore.

But the trail of acorn shells led on. Sophie looked ahead into the dense underbrush. She saw a few more shells and made her way to them. Then she saw more farther on.

What was Winston doing coming this way? Sophie wondered. *It's not easy getting through here. And it's kind of far from home. Where was he going?*

Sophie kept following the trail of acorn shells. She ducked under

thorny vines. She climbed over fallen branches. She squeezed through a tight space between two rocks. And she parted a curtain of ivy.

Then she stopped. She was staring at a door—a wooden door in the side of a rocky mound. It was mouse-size. And it had a knocker.

Sophie did what any adventurous mouse would do: She knocked on the door.

Within seconds, it swung open. On the other side was an old gray mouse. He was wearing suspender trousers, a button-down shirt, and

a wool cap. He was nibbling on
an acorn. Bits of shell fell onto the
doorstep.

The mouse pulled a pair of
glasses out of his shirt pocket. He
put them on and peered through
them at Sophie.

"What do you want?" he said, a bit grumpily.

For a moment Sophie was speechless. Then she blurted out, "You're not Winston!"

"Correct!" the old mouse said. "I'm not Winston!" And he shut the door firmly.

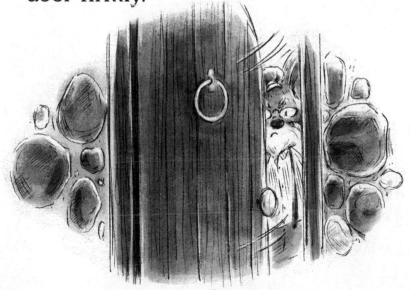

walking in circles

Sophie stood frozen to the spot. Her mouth hung open in surprise. She was too shocked to feel insulted.

She thought back to the toad reading the paper near Hattie's house. She said she'd seen a small gray mouse. And she had. It just wasn't Winston!

All this time, Sophie had been tracking the wrong mouse!

Sophie was worried. She realized she had no idea where Winston was. She was the one who had sent him home. And now he was missing. What if he was lost? Winston wasn't as good at finding his way around Silverlake Forest as she was.

Sophie looked up toward the sky. She sniffed the air. She saw moss growing on the north side of a tree trunk. She did some figuring in her head. She'd gone all the way from Butterfly

Brook, to her house, to the play-ground, to the stream. Then she had tracked the mouse to where she was now.

She realized she'd walked in one big circle! That meant she was not far from Butterfly Brook now.

Sophie made a decision. She had to tell her parents Winston was missing. Both of them were in town. The fastest way there would take her past Butterfly Brook. She'd stop on the way to tell Hattie and Owen what was going on.

Sophie set out at a quick pace. She really hoped her mom and dad knew what to do. As Sophie neared Butterfly Brook, she came to a mud puddle. A stick was standing straight up in the mud. Sophie hopped over the puddle and noticed some lines drawn in the mud. *That kind of looks like an* M, she thought as she hurried on.

Three steps later, Sophie stopped suddenly. She turned around and hurried back to the mud.

From this side, the *M* looked
like . . . a *W*! A *W* for Winston!
 Could Winston have drawn it?
Could he actually be nearby?

"WIN-ston?"

Sophie called out.

"WINSTON!"

But there was
no answer. All
Sophie heard were
birds chattering
above and her own
voice echoing off
the tree trunks all
around.

Sophie walked quickly on. She
zipped through a tunnel of low-
hanging branches. She darted
around a briar patch. She sped along

the edge of a gully. When her nose
caught the scent of water, she knew
she was almost at Butterfly Brook.

Then, around a bend in the path,
Sophie saw it. A square of white

fabric stood out on the dark forest floor. She picked it up.

It was her handkerchief! The one she had given Winston for his knee! Now Sophie was sure. *He must have been here,* Sophie thought. *But . . . this isn't the way home.*

Then a completely new idea came to her.

What if Winston didn't go home at all?

chapter 9

winston's surprise

Sophie's mind was racing. But before she could make sense of it all, she heard a sound. It was slow and steady. *Knock, knock, knock.* She listened, then followed the sound.

The sound got louder as Sophie got closer to the source. *Knock . . . knock . . . knock . . .*

Sophie came over a little rise.

On the other side was a small gray mouse. He was holding a rock in one hand. He was using it like a hammer to pound a stick into the ground.

"WINSTON!" Sophie cried.

She ran to her brother. Winston stopped hammering. He looked up, startled, as Sophie plowed into him.

She swept him up in a huge hug. Winston squirmed. But Sophie didn't let go.

"Oh Winston, you have no idea how glad I am to see you!"

"What are you doing?" Winston asked when he was finally able to

wriggle free. "What's the big deal?"

Sophie sighed with relief. Then she began talking very fast. "Winston, I'm *so* sorry I sent you home before. But I went home looking for you. Because we needed your help. And you weren't at the house. Now I know it's because you never went there. Hey . . . but that means

you didn't listen to me! Never mind. I'm not mad. I've been searching everywhere for you. And here you are! I'm so glad you're okay!"

Winston looked confused for a second. He was taking it all in. "Of course I'm okay," he said. He put his hands on his hips. "But why did you need my help?"

Sophie smiled. She opened her mouth to tell him how he

could save the day with his knot-
tying skills.

But before any words came out,
Sophie noticed something. Behind
Winston was a big structure. The
stick that Winston had been hammering was part of it—just one small
part.

Winston had built his own fort.
And it was an amazing fort!

Sophie gasped. "Winston, how
did you *do* this?" she
asked in wonder.

chapter 10

Go, Team!

Winston smiled proudly. "You like it?" he asked Sophie.

Sophie nodded, speechless, as she studied the fort. Winston had used rocks as his building blocks. He had used wet mud to hold the rocks in place. This was how he had built up the walls. Then he had layered pine boughs on top to make the roof.

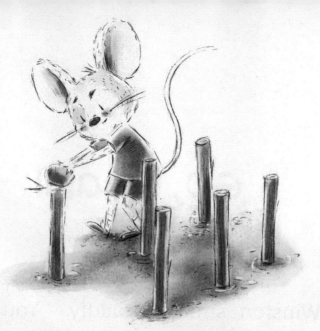

"I'm adding a front porch," said Winston. He picked up another stick. He hammered it into the ground with his rock.

"It's really, really cool," Sophie said, admiring it. "Can we show Hattie and Owen?"

Winston nodded. Sophie called

down toward the brook. "Hattie! Owen! Are you down there?"

Far off, Sophie heard their voices in reply. She called for them to come up. "You have to see this!" she shouted.

While they waited for Hattie and Owen, Sophie had an idea. But she wasn't sure what her brother would think of it.

"Um, Winston," she said timidly. "Do you need any

help? Because . . . I mean . . . if you *want*, we could help you finish your fort. We could build one giant fort together."

Winston stopped hammering.

"I don't *need* any help," he said.

Sophie's shoulders dropped. "Oh," she said sadly. "Okay. I understand if you want to do it yourself—"

Winston interrupted. "What I mean is, I *could* do it all by myself." He paused. "But if you *want* to help me, I guess you can. We could make a bigger and better fort if we worked together."

Sophie clapped in excitement. "Great!" she said. "It'll be so fun!"

Hattie and Owen came walking up. They were just as amazed by Winston's fort as Sophie was. And they hadn't gotten very far with their own fort, so they were happy to help Winston with his.

Winston worked on finishing the front porch. Owen and Hattie used Winston's extra rocks and mud to add another small room. Winston showed them how to tie the roof pieces together with super-strong knots! Sophie figured out how to put

a skylight in the roof. Then they all worked together to add a front door.

When they were done, they found rocks and bark pieces just the right

size for seats. They set them inside the fort in a circle. Then they sat down together. Sophie shared the water and snacks she had in her satchel.

"This is so cool!" said Winston. "Our own fort in the woods!"

"Wait until we tell Dad at dinner!" said Sophie. "He's going to be so proud of your building design, Winston!"

Sophie imagined painting a picture of her day after dinner. It would be a painting of their fort at Butterfly Brook. There would be blue morpho butterflies fluttering around. And her brother, Winston, would be right in the middle of the scene.

The End

Here's a peek at the next
Adventures of Sophie Mouse book!

Sophie Mouse tapped her pencil on her school desk. Her assignment was to write a math word-problem. Sophie wondered if Mrs. Wise would like hers.

Lily Mouse had 100 maple tarts to sell at the Maple Festival. She sold 20 before lunch. She sold 30 after lunch. How many did she have left to take home to her family?

Mmmm . . . thought Sophie as she reread the problem. Autumn was a very yummy time of year. It was when her mom made all kinds of maple treats at her bakery in Pine Needle Grove. And every year, Mrs. Mouse sold them at the big Maple Festival. Sophie couldn't wait for this year's festival. It was coming up next weekend!

A cool breeze blew in through the window. It carried a few red leaves with it.

"Okay, class!" Mrs. Wise called out. "Time for recess!"

The whole class jumped up. Sophie joined her friends Hattie Frog and Owen Snake at the door. They headed out to the playground.

"Are you both going to the Maple Festival this weekend?" Sophie asked them.

Hattie nodded. "Of course!" she said. "I want to ride the Ferris wheel at least five times!"

Owen gasped. "There will be a Ferris wheel?" His family had moved to Pine Needle Grove a few months before. He had never been to the Maple Festival.

"Owen, there's so much to do there!" Sophie cried. The three friends were nearing the swings. "There's dragonfly racing. You can play games to win prizes, like cranberry necklaces and acorn-top yo-yos!"

"There are ribbon-dancing grass-hoppers!" added Zoe, a bluebird who was swinging on a swing.

"And my mom's bake stand!" said Winston, Sophie's little brother. He ran between Sophie and Hattie and was gone in a flash.

"Yummm," said several students, rubbing their bellies.

the adventures of
SOPHIE MOUSE

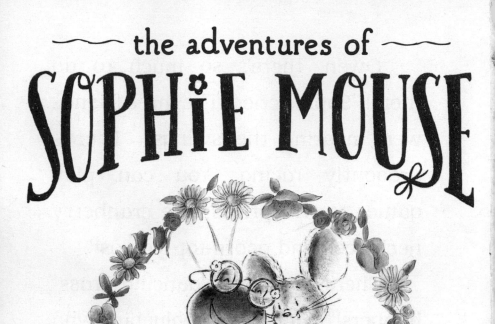

For excerpts, activities, and more about
these adorable tales & tails, visit
AdventuresofSophieMouse.com!